AMAZING ENERGY EXPERIMENTS

Q. L. PEARCE

Illustrated by
TONY GLEESON

A TOM DOHERTY ASSOCIATES BOOK
NEW YORK

SUPER SCIENCE EXPERIMENTS
published by Tor Books

Amazing Energy Experiments
Wondrous Plant and Earth Experiments

AMAZING ENERGY EXPERIMENTS

Copyright © 1989 by RGA Publishing Group

A TOR Book
Published by Tom Doherty Associates, Inc.
49 West 24 Street
New York, NY 10010

ISBN: 0-812-59387-1   Can. ISBN: 0-812-59388-X

First edition: September 1989

Book design by Stacey Simons/Neuwirth & Associates

Printed in the United States of America

0 9 8 7 6 5 4 3 2 1

Contents

NOTE TO PARENTS

Super Science Experiments/Physics is the perfect supplement to the classroom science curriculum. It is filled with hands-on experiments that will spark your child's interest and curiosity in his or her environment. Each activity has been designed to be safe and simple, requiring materials that are inexpensive and readily available. If possible, provide an area where often-used items may be stored. Some experiments may be a little messy. Those that involve heat or sharp instruments, perhaps requiring adult supervision or participation, are marked by asterisks.

At the beginning of the book, there is a list of materials needed for many of the experiments, followed by a section on safety sense. It is a good idea to review these segments with your child before he or she begins the first activity.

After an experiment has been completed, ask questions about how and why it worked as it did. Encouraging youngsters to formulate their own ideas will promote understanding of the basic concept illustrated by each activity.

ABOUT THIS BOOK . . .

Why do things work the way they do? Things happen for reasons that may not be clear at first. Men and women are working in every branch of science to discover the answers. The best way to find out is through observation and experimentation. First you must have a question; then you think of a way to find the answer. Each of the experiments that follow starts with a question. Read the activity through completely before you begin, and be sure you have all the materials at hand. Sometimes finding an answer will lead to more questions. If so, go ahead and design your own experiments and keep a notebook to record your results. Have fun!

YOUR SCIENCE LAB

The kitchen is the best place to perform most experiments. Certain things you will need, such as running water, are available. In some cases you may need to heat things on the stove or cool them in the refrigerator. Many of your supplies are probably in the home already. Ask an adult before you use household materials.

Here is a list of some of the items you may need for your physics laboratory:

- chopping board for cutting
- salt, food coloring, baking soda, vinegar, sugar, liquid detergent
- saucepan, pie plate, clean glass jam or jelly jars with lids, measuring cups, measuring spoons, wooden spoon, drinking glass, mixing bowls
- string, tape, paper clips, balloons, rubber bands, plastic straws, scissors, eyedropper, sieve, thermometer, stopwatch or clock with a second hand, scale, clothespins, wire cutters, rubber tubing
- pot holder, gloves, apron, newspaper, notebook, pencils, marking pen

For certain experiments, you may need some materials that are not mentioned here. Read through the list at the beginning of each activity before you begin.

SAFETY SENSE

Here are a few simple rules that you should *always* follow in your laboratory:

1. Read the experiment through completely before you begin.
2. Wear old clothing or an apron.
3. Cover your work area with newspaper.
4. Never put an unknown material in your mouth or near your eyes.
5. Clean your work area and instruments when you are finished.
6. Wash your hands after each experiment.
7. If an experiment will need a long time to finish, find a place where it will not be in the way of other family members.
8. For some experiments you may need help. These are marked with an asterisk (*).

What is science?

Science is the study of the universe and everything in it, big or small, new or old. One of the most basic of the sciences is physics. This is the study of the relationship between the matter and energy that make up our universe and the forces that affect them. Most other branches of science, including chemistry, geology, and astronomy, depend on the laws of physics. Here are a few of those laws that have been discovered and how they have been applied.

Light always travels at the same speed. Light travels through space at about 186,000 miles per second. If you know how long a beam of light takes to reach a certain point, you can figure out how far away that point is. During the Apollo Moon missions, special mirrors were positioned on the surface of the moon. Astronomers on earth were able to shoot a laser beam, bounce it off the moon mirrors and back to earth. By recording the amount of time it took for the beam to travel from the earth to the moon and back, they could figure out the exact distance between our planet and its satellite.

A body in motion will stay in motion unless it is acted on by a force. This law means that once something is moving, it will continue to move in the same direction and at the same speed unless something else stops it or changes its motion. Knowing this law helped scientists to plan the Voyager Space Probe's course to the outer planets. They knew that Voyager would keep moving outward but its course could be changed by the effect of the gravitational pull of planets as it flew by them.

A current of moving electrons produces a magnetic field. This knowledge led to the development of electromagnets (you'll get to make one of these later in the book). Electromagnets are used to do work in many ways, such as in the ignition systems in cars, in telephones and televisions, and in radar equipment.

There are natural magnets, too. Let's start our experiments by finding out about magnets and magnetism.

MAGNETS AND MAGNETISM

MAGNETIC POWERS

What do magnets attract?

Materials:

magnet
variety of objects, including paper, paper clips, pencil,
coins, scissors, plastic cup, bobby pins, steel straight
pins, needle, drinking glass, cardboard

Procedure:

1. Look at your objects. Separate them into two groups, one with things you think *will* be attracted by the magnet, and one with things you think *won't* be attracted.

2. Touch your magnet to each object. If your guess was correct, leave the object in that group. If you were wrong, place the object in the other group.

3. Look at the group of things that magnets attract. What is something that is alike about all of these items?

WHAT'S HAPPENING HERE? Magnets mainly attract metal objects containing iron, nickel, or cobalt.

HARD WORK

Can some things block out magnetism?

Materials:

magnet
handkerchief
paper
drinking glass

wooden ruler
aluminum
  cookie sheet
plastic cup

paper clip
stainless steel
  saucepan

Procedure:

1. Try to pick up each of the materials with the magnet. Do any of them "stick"?

2. Place a paper clip under a piece of paper. Using your magnet, touch the paper directly over the clip. Try lifting the paper at this spot. What happens?

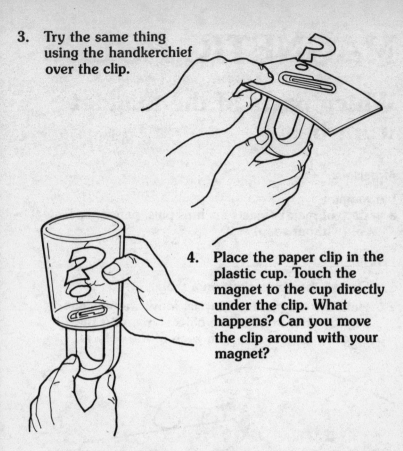

3. Try the same thing
    using the handkerchief
    over the clip.

4. Place the paper clip in the
    plastic cup. Touch the
    magnet to the cup directly
    under the clip. What
    happens? Can you move
    the clip around with your
    magnet?

5. Try the same thing using the glass. Try it with water
    in the glass, too. What happens?
6. Put the clip on the ruler. Put your magnet below it.
    Can your magnet move the clip through the wood?
    Now try the cookie sheet and the saucepan. Is there
    a difference?

WHAT'S HAPPENING HERE? The area around a
magnet in which its force can be felt is called its
magnetic field. The effect of the field on certain
objects depends on the strength and distance from
the object. The magnetic field can penetrate some
materials but not others.

MAGNETIC POLES

Which parts of the magnet work best?

Materials:

bar magnet
a variety of metal objects such as pins, paper clips, steel
   wool (without soap)

Procedure:

1. Spread the objects out on a table.
2. Hold the magnet lengthwise. Move the magnet
    slightly above one of the objects, then lift the
    magnet. Repeat this with each of the objects.

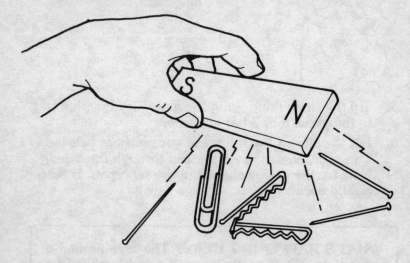

3. To which part of the magnet do most of the objects
    stick?
4. Which part of the magnet was strong enough to lift
    each of the materials? Are the ends (called poles) or
    the middle of the magnet stronger?

WHAT'S HAPPENING HERE? The force of a magnet is concentrated at its ends, or *poles*.

NORTH AND SOUTH

Are both magnetic poles the same?

Materials:

compass   2 bar magnets   string   crayon

Procedure:

1. Use the compass to find out which direction is due north.

2. Tie a piece of string around the center of your magnet so that it hangs level. Hold the loose end or tie it to something so that the magnet can spin freely. Which end or pole is pointing north when it stops turning? With the crayon, mark that end N for

north, and the other end S for south. (This is important to remember for further experiments.)

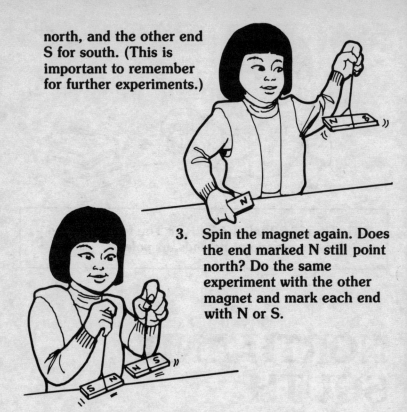

3. Spin the magnet again. Does the end marked N still point north? Do the same experiment with the other magnet and mark each end with N or S.

4. Hold the magnets so that both north poles are pointed toward each other. Do like poles attract each other or push each other away?

5. Point both south poles toward each other. What happens?

6. Remove the markings from one of the magnets. Now bring the two magnets close together. Are they attracted to each other or repelled? Can you guess which poles is which on the unmarked magnet by how it reacts to the marked one?

WHAT'S HAPPENING HERE? Unlike poles attract each other and like poles repel each other. In other words, opposites attract.

MAGNETIC FIELD*

What is a magnetic field shaped like?

*Materials:**

steel wool pads
old scissors
2 bar magnets with the poles labeled
a sheet of plain paper

Procedure:

1. Cut the steel wool into tiny bits with the scissors. Place the magnet on a table and hold the sheet of paper slightly above it. Sprinkle the steel wool bits on the paper. Does a pattern form?

2. Move the paper away from the magnet and gently shake it. Does the pattern disappear? Place the paper above the magnet again. What happens?

3. Move the paper away again, place the second magnet near the first with north and south poles facing each other, and hold the paper over both magnets. Is the pattern of the steel wool bits different this time?

4. Turn one magnet so that both north poles are facing each other. Does the pattern change?

WHAT'S HAPPENING HERE? The steel wool clippings are attracted to the lines of force, or magnetic field, around the magnet. The pattern you see is the shape of the magnetic field.

FUN WITH MAGNETS

Magnets can be used to make work easier by pushing and pulling heavy loads. Sometimes magnets can keep things in place, and magnets are used in some modern trains to move cars of people safely from place to place.

Here are some things you can make that use magnets.

MAGNETIC PUPPET SHOW

Materials:

lightweight	scissors	tape
cardboard	crayons and	paper clips
shoe box	marking pens	2 bar magnets

1. Prepare your stage by cutting out one side of the shoe box. Turn the box upside down and make one inch cuts along each back edge as illustrated. Draw a scene on the inside of the lid and color it. Now slip the lid into the cuts you made and tape it securely.

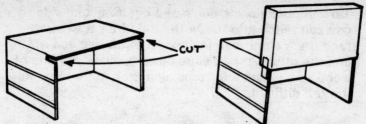

2. Draw two characters on the cardboard and color each. Cut them out, leaving a tab of cardboard at the bottom. Fold the tab so that each figure can stand up, and slip a paper clip over each tab.

3. Place your characters on the stage. By moving the bar magnets in the shoe box, you can make the figures move and act out a story.

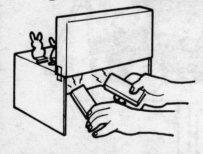

MAGNET RACERS

Materials:

cardboard box	pebbles and bits	large paper clip
scissors	of wood	bar magnet
marking pen	glue	stopwatch
	cardboard	

1. Turn the box upside down and cut away one side so you can reach into it. On the top, draw a twisting race track about one inch wide. Mark one end START and the other FINISH. Glue down pebbles and bits of wood as barriers and traps along the route to make it more difficult.

2. Fold a piece of cardboard and draw a race car on one side with the top along the fold. Color and cut out the car.

3. Pull up the center of the paper clip and twist it until it looks like the one in the illustration. Slide your car over the clip and glue it together.

4. Place the car at the beginning of the track. Use the magnet under the box to move the car along. Start the stopwatch and see how long it takes you to complete the track. Take turns racing with your friends to see who can make the best time.

ELECTRICITY

CHARGE IT

Do electrically charged objects attract nonmetal objects?

Materials:

plastic comb   small bits of paper   wool fabric

Procedure:

1. Hold the comb over the small pieces of paper for a moment. Does anything happen? Turn on the kitchen tap slowly so that there is a steady stream of water. Hold the comb as close to the stream as you can without getting it wet. Does anything happen now?

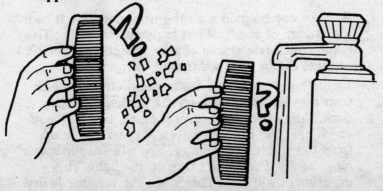

2.   Rub the comb briskly with the wool fabric.

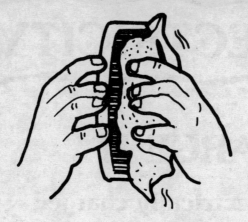

3. Hold it over the pieces of paper. They stick to the comb.

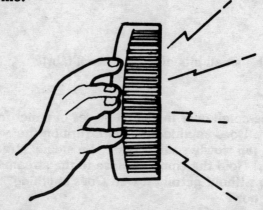

4. Rub the comb again with the wool and hold it near the stream of water. What happens this time? The comb contains a stored charge of *static electricity*. It attracts things with a different charge.

5. Lightning is caused by static electricity. To make your own lightning turn on the kitchen tap after dark. Comb your hair several times, then place the comb near the running water. A spark will jump from the comb to the water. You will see the spark more easily if you don't turn on the light. This experiment will work best when the weather is dry.

WHAT'S HAPPENING HERE? One of the most basic properties of electricity is *charge*. Charge can be negative or positive. Objects with opposite charge are attracted to each other and those with like charge repel. Electrons have a negative charge. They are tiny particles that orbit the center of atoms. Protons (tiny particles in the center of atoms) have a positive charge. An atom with fewer electrons than protons is positively charged. An atom with more electrons than protons is negatively charged. Atoms with an even number of both are *neutral*. Static electricity is the buildup of either negative or positive charge in a substance.

LIKE MAGIC

Can static electricity do work?

Materials:

5 by 5 inch square of paper	1 sharp pencil	thread
	comb	2 balloons
scissors	piece of wool fabric	
modeling clay		

Procedure:

1. Fold the paper and cut it as shown in the drawing to form a star. Push the eraser end of the pencil into the ball of clay so it will stand. Balance the paper star on the point of the pencil.

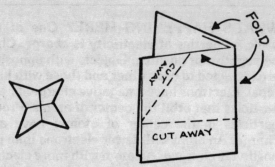

2. Run the comb through your hair several times or rub it with the fabric. Hold the comb near but not touching the star and make a circle around it. The star will begin to move. Do you know what is causing it to spin?

3. Hold a piece of thread in one hand. With the other hand, comb your hair quickly, then pass the comb over the thread. It will rise up and follow the comb. The thread is attracted to the comb.

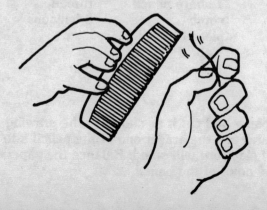

4. Blow up both balloons and tie one to each end of a **15** long piece of thread. Holding the thread in the center allow the balloons to dangle. Do they touch? Quickly rub each balloon on your hair. Dangle the balloons again. Will they touch each other now?

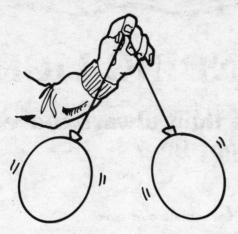

WHAT'S HAPPENING HERE? Protons always stay in the same place, but electrons can be made to move from one atom to another. Between certain materials, electrons move very easily. By running the comb through your hair or rubbing the balloons together, you are causing electrons to move from one place to another. The objects build up either a positive or negative charge depending on the materials you use.

LIGHT

BENDING LIGHT

Does light always move in a straight line?

Materials:

square glass container or tank
pencil
large piece of white cardboard or paper
flashlight
milk

Procedure:

1. Fill the tank with water. Hold the pencil half in and half out of the water. Does it appear to bend?

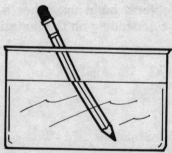

2. Look at the pencil from different angles. Does the pencil seem to change depending on how you look at it? Look at it from directly above. Does the part in the water appear closer than it should be?

3. Remove the pencil. Hold the white paper about an inch from one side of the tank. On the opposite side, hold the flashlight straight and shine it directly through the water at the paper. The beam will not appear to bend.

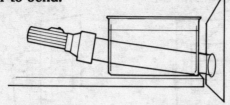

4. Tilt the flashlight slightly upward. Does the beam bend? Which way does it bend? Add a little milk to the water and the light beam will be seen more clearly.

WHAT'S HAPPENING HERE? As light rays travel from air to water or water to air at certain angles, they are slowed and bent slightly. This is called *refraction*.

ENERGY YOU CAN SEE

What color is light?

Materials:

tall glass   3 by 5 inch index card   scissors
tape   large sheet of white paper

Procedure:

1. A beam of white light is made up of many colors that our brain perceives as one. To break a beam of

light into its individual colors cut a one-inch-wide three-inch-long rectangle from a white 3 by 5 inch index card with the scissors.

2. Tape the card to the glass so that the opening is directly over the rim.

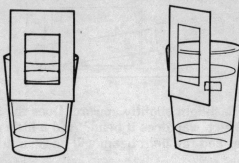

3. Fill the glass with water and set it on the ledge or on a table in front of a sunny window. Place the white paper on the floor in front of the glass. The colors will be reflected individually on the white card under the glass. How many colors do you see? These colors make up the *visible spectrum*.

WHAT'S HAPPENING HERE? Sunlight is made up of many different colors of light. Each of these different colors vibrate at a slightly different speed. When the sunlight passes through the water in the glass, each of the colors is slowed and bent. The colors that vibrate faster are bent more than the colors that vibrate slower. Blue and violet rays bend the most, and red the least.

FUN WITH LIGHT

Sometimes light does not pass through an object, but is bounced back. This is called *reflection*. Mirrors can be used to bounce light rays. Follow these directions to make your own periscope and you will be able to see around corners!

*UP PERISCOPE**

*Materials:**

quart milk carton
scissors
2 square pocket mirrors that fit inside the carton
tape

Procedure:

1. Clean out the milk carton carefully.
2. Cut the carton in half. In each half, cut a small hole near the bottom. Slip in a mirror and tape it faceup at about a 45 degree angle slanting toward the hole.

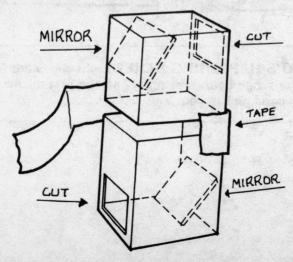

3. Tape the carton securely together again so that one hole is at the top of one side and the other hole is at the bottom of the opposite side.

4. Kneel down behind a chair and aim one hole over the back. Look through the other hole. What do you see?

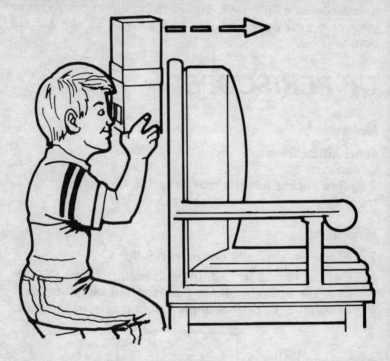

WHAT'S HAPPENING HERE? Light rays entering the periscope bounce or *reflect* off the first mirror to the second and to your eye.

HEAT

THE HEAT IS ON*

What is friction?

Materials:

2 dry sticks of wood, about 8 inches long and 1 inch
  thick
shoe box without lid
scissors
3 feet of string
brick

Procedure:

1. Hold the two sticks by the ends, one stick in each
    hand. Cross the sticks over each other and rub back
    and forth as hard as you can about twenty or thirty
    times.

2. Stop and feel the area
    that has been rubbed
    together. Is it warm?

3. With the scissors make a small hole in the short side of the shoe box. Tie one end of the string through the hole. Use the string to pull the empty box across a hard surface on the ground such as a sidewalk. Walk slowly back and forth a few times, pulling the box behind you.

4. Stop. Feel the bottom of the box. Is it warm? Wait a moment, then do the experiment again but this time run back and forth quickly. Is there a difference? Put the brick in the box and repeat both steps. Is the bottom of the box warm? Are the sides warm?

WHAT'S HAPPENING HERE? Most surfaces are rough and do not slide easily past each other. If you could look at them through a microscope you would see that even things that seem to be smooth, such as metal or glass, are actually rough. This resistance when you rub surfaces together is called *friction*. It takes energy to make the surfaces move across each other and much of that energy is turned into heat. Spacecraft returning to Earth through the atmosphere heat up because of friction with the air.

KEEPING COOL*

Can friction be controlled?

*Materials:**

2 blocks of wood about 3 inches square
soap
2 metal jar lids
cooking oil

Procedure:

Procedure:

1. Create friction by rubbing the two blocks of wood together very quickly for a few moments. Feel them. Do they feel warm?

2. Smear soap between the blocks, then rub them together again. Feel them. Did they heat up? Why not? When things slide past each other more easily do they create less heat?

3. Rub the metal lids together. They appear very smooth. Do they heat up? Rub a little oil between the lids then try again. Did they heat up as much?

WHAT'S HAPPENING HERE? The soap and oil are *lubricants*. Lubricants are substances used to coat the surfaces between moving objects so that they slide past each other more easily. Lubricants can help prevent machine parts from wearing out.

EXPAND OR CONTRACT*

What happens when a gas becomes hotter?

Materials:

nail
bottle with a
   plastic
   screw-on cap

food coloring
drinking straw
clay

container large
   enough to hold
   the bottle

Procedure:

1. With the nail make a hole in the bottle cap large enough for the straw to fit through. Fill the bottle halfway with water and add a few drops of food coloring.

2. Screw on the cap, and slide the straw until it is about an inch from the bottom of the bottle. Seal around the cap's edges with clay and plug the hole of the straw too, but make a small hole in the center of the clay with the nail. Do you think you can get the water out of the bottle without tipping it over or taking off the cap?

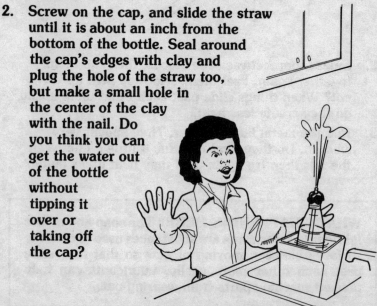

3. Place the container in the sink because this can be a little messy. Fill the container with very hot water and put the bottle in it. Wait until the air in the bottle warms up. What happens?

WHAT'S HAPPENING HERE? Most things expand or get larger when they heat up. As the warm air in the bottle expanded, it pushed down on the water. This caused some of the water to travel up the straw and spray out of the top of the bottle.

THE BIG STORY*

Do solids expand when heated?

*Materials:**

1 piece of wood about 8 inches long, 6 inches wide, and ½ inch thick (piece A)	2 pieces of wood about 4 by 4 inches and ½ inch thick (pieces B and C) nails	aluminum rod about 1 foot long crayon, pen or pencil 3 candles

Procedure:

1. Ask your adult helper to drill a hole in one of the smaller pieces of wood (piece B); then nail the three pieces together as in the illustration, with piece A on the bottom.

2. Fit the aluminum rod into the hole in piece B. Rest the end on a nail driven into piece C. Make a mark on the wood at the end of the rod.

3. Measure the distance between piece A and the rod. Cut the candles one inch shorter than this distance. Place the three candles under the metal rod and light them.

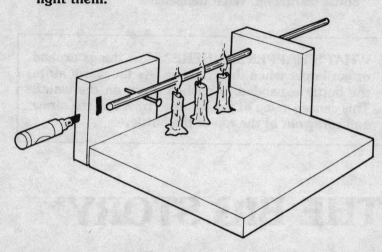

4. After a few minutes compare the end of the rod with your mark. Is the rod longer? Did the heat from the candles cause it to expand? Make a new mark at the end of the rod and remove the candles.

5. After the metal has cooled completely check the mark again. What happened?

WHAT'S HAPPENING HERE? When most materials are heated, the atoms that they are made of move farther apart. This causes the material to expand.

SOUND

DID YOU HEAR THAT?

What is sound?

Materials:

balloon	rubber band	small mirror
can opener	sugar	tape
coffee can with	saucepan	flashlight
both ends	metal spoon	
removed		

Procedure:

1. Cut the bottom of a coffee can. Cut the balloon and stretch it across the top of the opened can. Secure it with a rubber band. Place a teaspoon of sugar in the center. Now holding the saucepan close to the can, bang on it with the spoon. Does the sugar move?

2. Remove the sugar and tape the mirror to the balloon, shiny side up.

3. Set the can on its side on a tabletop. Prop a flashlight in front of it so that the light reflects from the mirror on to the opposite wall.

4. Sing into the back of the can. What happens to the light? Why is it vibrating?

WHAT'S HAPPENING HERE? Sound is the vibration of molecules (usually air molecules). These vibrations travel in waves. You can actually see the effect the vibrations have on the balloon stretched across the coffee can. What do you think would happen to sound in a place without air molecules such as outer space?

HIGH OR LOW

Why are some sounds higher than others?

Materials:

ruler   book   rubber band   2 small erasers

Procedure:

1. Place the ruler on the table with about nine inches beyond the edge and hold it there. Put the book on top of it to hold it in place. Pull down on the end and let it flick up again. Did it make a noise?

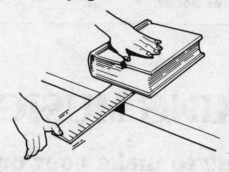

2. Push the ruler two inches farther under the book and flick it again. Was the noise higher or lower than the first sound? Push the ruler in two more inches and try it again. As the exposed end gets shorter, what happens to the sound it makes?

3. Pick up the ruler and stretch a rubber band over it lengthwise. Slip an eraser under the band at each end. Pluck at the rubber band. Move the erasers closer together and pluck at the rubber band again. The faster something vibrates the higher the sound. When you shorten the rubber band is it vibrating faster or slower? How do you know?

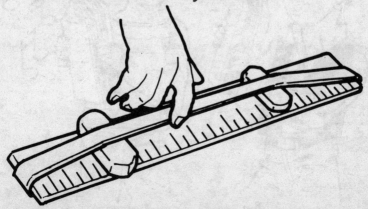

WHAT'S HAPPENING HERE? Sound waves vibrate at different speeds. Waves that vibrate fast have a higher pitch than waves that vibrate slowly. The shorter that you make the rubber band, the faster the sound waves vibrate.

MAKING MUSIC

It's easy to make your own musical instrument.

Materials:

½ gallon milk carton   scissors   pencil
several long thick and thin rubber bands   tape

Procedure:

1. Cut a hole about three inches wide and four inches long in one side of the milk carton. Tape a pencil across the bottom edge of the hole.

2. Stretch the rubber bands lengthwise around the carton so that part of each one is over the hole, just like in the picture. Put them in order, thick to thin.

3. Each band will have a different sound when you pluck it. You can change its sound by holding the band against the milk carton. This will make the "string" shorter. Will the new sound be higher or lower?

GRAVITY

In science fiction stories, you often hear about "force fields." There are force fields in real life too, such as Earth's magnetic field. Can you think of another force that is very important? It keeps the planets in orbit and holds everything on Earth, even the atmosphere, in place . . . the force is gravity.

HOLD TIGHT

Does gravity pull harder on bigger objects?

Materials:

book   large sponge   tennis ball
rock the size of a tennis ball   scale

Procedure:

1. Hold the book in your outstretched hand. Can you feel gravity pulling down on it. What will happen if you let go of the book?
2. Try lifting the sponge. It is much lighter. Is gravity pulling down on it? Let go of it. What happens?
3. Hold the tennis ball and the rock in your hand. Upon which object does gravity seem to be pulling

harder? Does gravity pull harder on objects only
because of their size? Is there another difference
between the rock and the tennis ball? Weigh each
object.

WHAT'S HAPPENING HERE? Size alone does not
determine how hard gravity pulls on an object. An
object's *mass* is more important. Mass is the amount
of particles such as protons, neutrons, and electrons
that make up the molecules in a substance. *Weight* is
the measure of the pull of gravity on mass. If two
objects are the same size and one is heavier, it is more
massive.

FALLING OBJECTS

Do objects of different sizes and weights fall at different speeds?

Materials:

scale	ball of crumpled	block of wood
tennis ball	aluminum foil	large book
rubber ball	large marble	sheet of paper
	baseball	

Procedure:

1. Weigh each of the objects. Are they all different?
   Stand and hold the tennis ball and the rubber ball at
   the same level. Drop them to the floor. Do they hit
   at the same time? Try dropping them from various
   heights but be sure they always start even.

2. Try the experiments with different combinations of balls. Do they always reach the ground at the same time no matter what size they are?

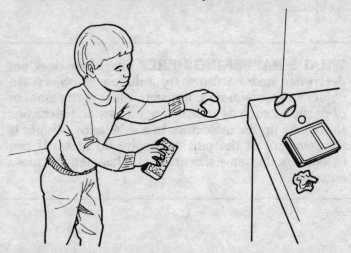

3. Drop a ball and the square block of wood. Do they hit at the same time? Does it matter that these objects are a different shape?

4. Drop the book and the paper at the same time. It takes longer for the paper to fall because friction with the air is slowing it down.

5. Crumple the paper into a tight ball. Now does it fall at the same rate as the book? What changed about the paper to prevent the air from slowing it down? Does shape have an effect on the rate of fall of certain objects?

WHAT'S HAPPENING HERE? The speed at which objects fall to the ground in a vacuum (an empty space that does not contain any air or any other mass) is the same no matter what the weight of the object. Objects falling through air may be slowed because of their shape. Friction with the air caused the flat piece of paper to fall more slowly. If you crumple the paper into a ball, you lessen this effect.

PERFECTLY BALANCED

What is a center of gravity?

Materials:

potato   pencil   2 forks   soda bottle

Procedure:

1. Cut a one-inch-thick slice from the center of the potato. Push the pencil through the potato slice about ½ inch from the edge so that it looks like the one in the picture. Try to balance the tip of the pencil off the edge of a table. Will it balance? Is the weight of the potato making it fall?

2. Push a fork into the lower edge of the potato so that it extends underneath the tabletop as in the illustration. Can you make it balance now? You may have to adjust it a few times until you finally get it to balance. Did you change the center of gravity of the object? How?

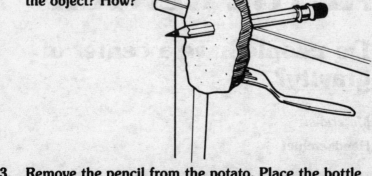

3. Remove the pencil from the potato. Place the bottle in the center of the table. Try to balance the pencil on its tip on top of the bottle. Now push the pencil through the center of the potato slice. Insert two forks into the edge directly opposite each other and

try it again. Can you make up some of your own balancing acts?

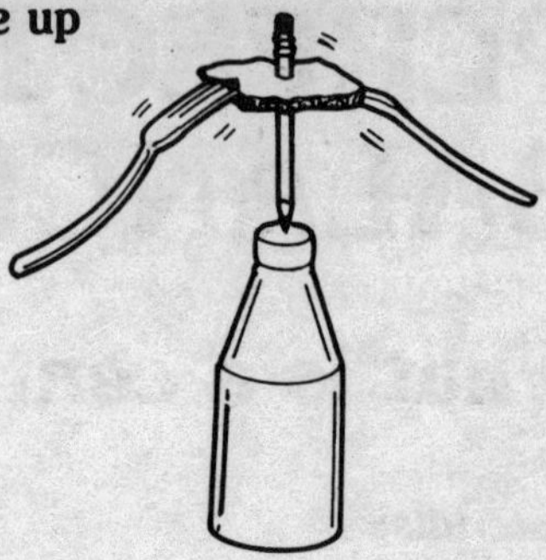

WHAT'S HAPPENING HERE? All things have a balance point or *center of gravity* at which they are balanced and do not fall. The potato slice has a center of gravity. When you add the pencil, you add weight to one side and change the balance point. By adding the fork to the other side, you change the center of gravity again.

AT THE CENTER

Do people have a center of gravity?

Materials:

Handkerchief

Procedure:

1. Stand in the middle of the room. Drop the handkerchief in front of you. Without bending your knees, lean over and pick up the handkerchief.

2. Stand with your back against a wall and try the experiment again. Is it harder this time? Do you lose your balance? Why?

3. Stand in the center of the room and lift your left foot out to the side. Does your body tip slightly to the right to adjust?

4. Try to do the same thing while standing with your right shoulder and foot against a wall. Can you lift your left foot now?

WHAT'S HAPPENING HERE? People have a center of gravity, too. When you are standing still you are balanced over your center of gravity. If you move a part of your body, without thinking about it you automatically make other movements to adjust to the new center. When you bend to pick up the handkerchief, you also shift your weight back a little to stay in balance. With your back against the wall you cannot shift your weight and so you lose your balance.

AIR

TEST OF STRENGTH

What is air pressure?

Materials:

glass
square of smooth cardboard bigger than the rim of the
   glass

Procedure:

1. Fill the glass with water and cover it with the
    cardboard. Be sure the cardboard is stiff and flat or
    the experiment will not work. Hold the cardboard in
    place with your hand. Standing with your hands
    over a large sink or bathtub (or outside in the yard)
    turn the glass over.

2. Remove your hand. What
    happens? Does the cardboard
    stay in place? Is the force of
    the air pushing up greater
    than the weight of the water?

3. What will happen if you move the cardboard enough to let air into the glass? Try it.

WHAT'S HAPPENING HERE? The air around us exerts a force on everything it touches. This force is called *air pressure*. The air pressure pushing up against the cardboard is greater than the weight of the water inside the glass.

ROOM FOR CHANGE*

What happens when air is heated or cooled?

*Materials:**

saucepan	candle about 3	quart jar
balloon	inches tall	marking pen
empty soda	shallow bowl	
bottle		

Procedure:

1. Ask your adult helper to fill a saucepan with very hot water. Slip the neck of the balloon over the rim of the soda bottle and place the bottle in the water. What happens as the air in the bottle heats up? How can you tell?

2. Ask your adult helper to light the candle and drip a little wax into the center of the bowl. Stand the candle up in the wax. Fill the bowl halfway with very cold water. Place the jar slowly upside down over the lit candle and mark the level of the water.

3. Wait until the candle goes out, then lightly touch the side of the jar. Is it warm? Is the air inside warm? After fifteen minutes or so, touch the jar again. Is it cool? Do you think the air inside is cool? Check the water level mark. Is the water higher or lower inside the jar?

WHAT'S HAPPENING HERE? In the first experiment, when you warm the air inside the bottle it expands or takes up more space. The warm air forced from the bottle goes into the balloon. In the second experiment, you warm the air first, then allow it to cool. As it cools it contracts or takes up less space. The outside air is pushing down on the water and some is forced up into the jar.

HEAVYWEIGHT

Does air have weight?

Materials:

string   light, plastic ruler   2 large balloons   pin

1. Tie a string in the center of the ruler, then hang it so it is level.
2. Blow up both balloons to exactly the same size, then tie off the end of each with a piece of string. Hang one balloon from each end of the ruler, adjusting the strings to make the ruler level again and so the balloons are completely balanced.
3. Let the air out of one balloon by bursting it with a pin. What happens to the ruler. Why? What happens if you burst the other balloon?

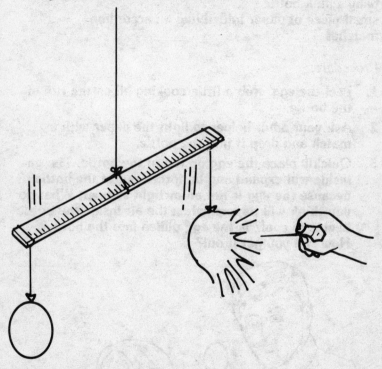

WHAT'S HAPPENING HERE? Air has weight. With an air-filled balloon on each end of the ruler, it is in balance. If you burst one balloon, the ruler will no longer be in balance and will be pulled down on one side by the weight of the air in the other balloon.

THE EGG AND I*

Can a change in air pressure create a pulling force?

*Material:**

1 small hard-boiled egg
cooking oil
baby's milk bottle
small piece of paper folded like an accordion
matches

Procedure:

1. Peel the egg. Rub a little cooking oil on the rim of the bottle.
2. Ask your adult helper to light the paper with a match and drop it into the bottle.
3. Quickly place the egg on top of the bottle. The gas inside will expand and be forced out of the bottle because the egg is not an airtight stopper. What do you think will happen when the air inside the bottle begins to cool? Is the egg pulled into the bottle? How can you get it out?

4. Tip the bottle upside down, push the egg aside, and blow into the bottle as hard as you can. Now hold out your hand and the egg will pop out into it.

WHAT'S HAPPENING HERE? The heated air in the bottle expands and much of it is forced out. As the bottle cools, there is less air within and so the pressure is lower inside the bottle than outside. Since the egg is not a perfect seal, outside air is drawn into the bottle and the egg is sucked in along with it. By blowing into the bottle you increase the air pressure inside. There is no longer room for the egg, so it pops out again.

UP WE GO*

How do airplanes stay up in the air?

*Materials:**

scissors   notebook paper   ruler

1. Cut a lengthwise strip from the notebook paper, about two inches wide.

2. Hold the paper in front of you with one of the ends near your mouth. Blow steadily straight ahead and across the top of the strip. What happens to the loose end?

WHAT'S HAPPENING HERE? The paper you are holding curves downward. When you blow across it, the air above the paper is moving faster than the air below it. The molecules of the air above the curved surface have a little farther to go than those passing across the flat surface underneath so they spread out a little and the air also becomes thinner. Because of this the air pressure is less above than below the paper. The slower more dense air pushes up with more pressure and the paper moves upward. This is called *lift*. The wings of an airplane are curved on top to help create lift.

WATER

WATERY FORCE

Does water exert pressure?

Materials:

large nail   2 milk cartons   tape

Procedure:

1. With the nail make three small holes in the side of the carton from top to bottom. Cover the holes with a strip of tape. Put the carton in the sink and fill it with water.

2. Remove the tape. Which stream is strongest and goes farther? Is the lowest hole under most pressure? Why?

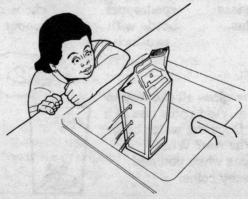

3. Set up the second carton as you did the first, but fill it only halfway with water. Refill the first.

4. Strip away tape from both. Which stream goes farther? Does the amount of water have an effect?

5. Punch a hole in each of the other sides. Does water pressure work in every direction?

WHAT'S HAPPENING HERE? Water has weight. The water in this experiment is pushing down and outward against the sides of the carton. Because of the weight of all the water above it, the water pressure is highest at the bottom of the carton. The stream at the bottom is pushed out with the most force and will spray farther than the stream at the top.

TOUGH SKIN

Why does water form drops?

Materials:

drinking glass	eyedropper	cheesecloth
6 or 7 coins	bottle with	rubber band
	two-inch rim	

Procedure:

1. Fill the glass all the way to the rim. Add coins one at a time. Does the water bulge over the rim? What happens when you add too many coins?

2. Fill the eyedropper with water and place one drop at
   a time on a smooth surface. Does the water tend to
   bead up?

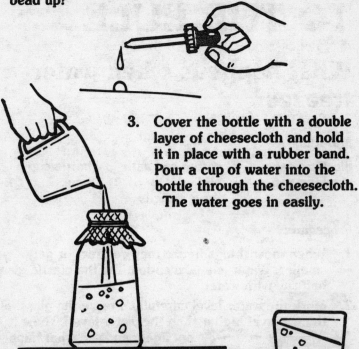

3. Cover the bottle with a double
   layer of cheesecloth and hold
   it in place with a rubber band.
   Pour a cup of water into the
   bottle through the cheesecloth.
   The water goes in easily.

4. Turn the bottle straight upside down
   over a sink. What happens? If the
   water went in through the cheesecloth,
   why doesn't it come out?

WHAT'S HAPPENING HERE? The water molecules
at the surface of the water are very strongly attracted
to each other and form a sort of "skin" across the
surface. This is called *surface tension*. It is surface
tension that causes water to form drops.

AN EXCEPTION TO THE RULE

What happens when water freezes?

Materials:

plastic glass	coffee can with	bottle cap
marking pen	lid	tape
	three pencils	

Procedure:

1. When most things freeze they contract or get smaller. Water is an exception. Fill the plastic glass halfway with water.

2. Mark the water level carefully. Freeze the glass. Is the ice level higher than the water level? Thaw it out again and see what happens.

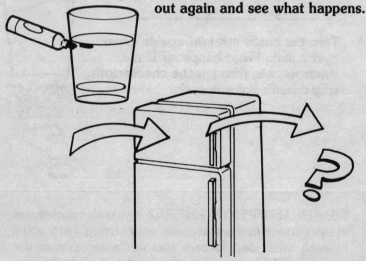

3. Fill the coffee can to the rim with cold water and cover it. Place the can on top of two of the pencils

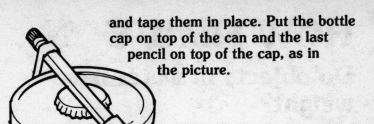

and tape them in place. Put the bottle **49**
cap on top of the can and the last
pencil on top of the cap, as in
the picture.

4. Tape all of the pencils tightly to each other by
   running a circle of tape around the point of the top
   pencil, then each bottom pencil and back to the top.
   Attach a circle of tape around the eraser end of the
   pencils, too. The pencils should not be able to move.
   You may need a friend to help you with this.

5. Place the coffee can in the freezer overnight. When
   you remove it, you will find that the pencil on the
   top has broken. Why?

WHAT'S HAPPENING HERE? When water freezes,
the molecules rearrange in such a way that there is
more space between them than when they are in
liquid form. Because of this, water expands when it
freezes. The ice in the can pushed up on the bottle cap
and snapped the pencil.

HOW HEAVY

Do objects in water have weight?

Materials:

pencil	ruler	small stone	metal bolt
tape	string	cork	small piece of wood
			2 plastic glasses

Procedure:

1. Tape the pencil down on a flat surface. Place the center of the ruler across the pencil. Put a glass on each end of the ruler and fill them both with water to about two inches from the rim. Balance carefully until both ends of the ruler are off the surface.

2. Place your finger in one glass. Does the weight of your finger tip the ruler off balance?

3. Using a small piece of string, suspend different objects in one glass—a piece of wood, a metal bolt, a stone, a cork. What happens?

4. Does the water level change depending on the weight of the object in the water? Which causes the water level to rise higher when in the glass—the cork or the stone?

WHAT IS HAPPENING HERE? When you put anything in the glass, the water is pushed aside or *displaced* by the object. The object then takes up the space and weighs the same as the water it has displaced. Since the water has only been moved and is still in the glass, its weight is also still felt, so the glass of water with your finger in it weighs a little more and will tip the ruler.

USING ENERGY AND FORCE

WATER MACHINE*

Can water be made to do work?

Materials:

plastic bottle scissors round file string
fishing swivel (available at sporting goods stores)

Procedure:

1. Cut the top of the bottle away.
   With the scissors, carefully
   make several holes about
   one inch apart at the bottom
   edge of the bottle and two holes
   at the top edge. File the holes at
   an angle so the edges are
   slightly slanted.

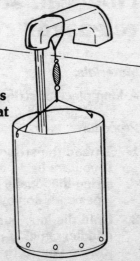

52   2.   Tie a piece of string between the holes at the top.
           Tie another string at the center of the first. Halfway
           up the center string, cut and tie in a fishing swivel.
           Reattach the string at the top of the swivel and tie
           the loose end to the faucet in the sink. Turn on a
           stream of water.

WHAT'S HAPPENING HERE? You have made a
water turbine. The water rushes out of the holes at
the bottom of the bottle, causing it to turn. It will turn
as long as water pours through it. This turbine could
move gears and wheels. A turbine in a moving river
would be a good source of energy.

ON HOLD

How can stored energy be released?

Materials:

A long piece of string   a one-inch-wide button

Procedure:

1.   Thread the string through both holes in the button.
     If you are using a button with four holes, thread the
     string diagonally through two of them only. Tie the
     loose ends so you have made a complete loop.
2.   Hold the loop outstretched with the button in the
     middle. Quickly make circles with both hands
     toward you so that the button spins around and the
     two rows of string twist together.

3. Pull on both ends of the string. It will untwist and the button will spin in the other direction. When you relax your hold, it will spin back again.

> **WHAT'S HAPPENING HERE?** The button is storing and releasing energy. By pulling on the string you are supplying more energy, which the button stores and then releases when you relax. You have made something called a *flywheel*.

POWER BOAT

How can released energy make an object move?

Materials:

plastic bottle	drinking straw	tissue paper
with screw-on	clay	½ cup vinegar
cap	3 tablespoons	
scissors	baking soda	

Procedure:

1. Make a hole in the bottom of the bottle, near the edge. Slide the straw into the hole so that only

about one inch sticks out. Pack the hole tightly around the straw with clay. Tilt the straw slightly so that it will be underwater when the bottle is placed in water.

2. Put 3 tablespoons of baking soda in a small square of tissue and roll it to form a tube. Twist both ends tightly shut. Place this in the bottle.

3. Pour ½ cup of vinegar in the bottle, screw on the cap, then set the bottle on its side in a sink about half full of water. Make sure the straw is underwater. What happens? What is causing the boat to move? What happens when it runs out of "fuel"?

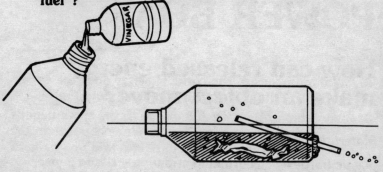

WHAT'S HAPPENING HERE? Inside the bottle the baking soda and vinegar combine to form carbon dioxide gas. As the gas escapes through the straw it pushes against the water, causing the boat to move forward.

FIRE THE CANNON

Can expanding gas move an object through air?

Materials:

1 teaspoon baking soda tissue paper	½ cup vinegar ½ cup water	bottle with cork 3 pencils

Procedure:

1. Wrap 1 teaspoon of baking soda in the tissue paper. Twist the ends to keep it shut. Put this in the bottle and add ½ cup vinegar and ½ cup water. Cork the bottle and wait.

2. What happens to the cork? How far does the cork go? Would it go farther if you used more fuel?

3. Lay the bottle on its side on top of the three pencils. Perform the experiment again. What happens to the bottle when the cork flies out? Why did you need to use the pencils?

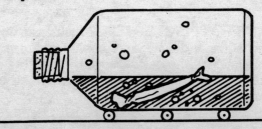

56

WHAT'S HAPPENING HERE? In the first experiment the expanding gas pushes against the cork and forces it out of the bottle. The second part of the experiment is an example of an important scientific law: *Every action has an equal and opposite reaction.* This means that every time an action takes place (the cork flying from the bottle), an equal but opposite reaction takes place (the bottle rolling backward). We used the pencils to make the reaction more obvious.

GLOSSARY

Science Words You Should Know

atmosphere	the layer of air around the Earth
atom	the smallest unit of an element that still behaves like the element
contract	to become smaller
condensation	changing of water vapor into a liquid, usually by cooling
conduction	transferring heat or electricity or other forms of energy from one place to another
density	the weight of an object or substance compared to the amount of space it occupies
electron	a very tiny particle of matter that contains a negative charge and usually orbits around the center of an atom
energy	the ability to do work
expand	to become larger
friction	the resistance to movement between one object and another as their surfaces pass each other
lubricant	a substance used to reduce friction
machine	a device used to do work
mass	the amount of matter in a substance

matter   the substance of which everything in the universe is made

molecule   the smallest particle of a substance that can exist alone and has all of the characteristics of that substance. Molecules are made up of atoms.

nucleus   the center of an atom, containing protons and neutrons

propulsion   a force that pushes an object forward

surface tension the force produced by the thin film at the surface of a liquid

solution   one or more substances dissolved in another, usually liquid, substance

vapor   a substance that is in a gaseous form

vibration   a rapid movement back and forth or up and down

volume   the amount of space an object or substance occupies